For my parents

ACKNOWLEDGMENTS

Frankenstink! was inspired by the movie and comic book creations of master monster-makers such as Ray Harryhausen, Jack Kirby, Wally Wood and Will Elder. Their imaginative stories and creatures sparked many of my childhood artistic efforts. My parents indulged my endless appetite for this glorious trash, so I gratefully dedicate this book to them.

Published in Canada by Tundra Books, a division of Random House of Canada Limited,
One Toronto Street, Suite 300, Toronto, Ontario M5C 2V6

Published in the United States by Tundra Books of Northern New York,
P.O. Box 1030, Plattsburgh, New York 12901

Library of Congress Control Number: 2014934269

Library and Archives Canada Cataloguing in Publication

Lightburn, Ron, author, illustrator
      Frankenstink! : garbage gone bad / written and illustrated by
Ron Lightburn.

Issued in print and electronic formats.
ISBN 978-1-77049-694-1 (bound).—ISBN 978-1-77049-696-5 (epub)

     I. Title.

PS8623.I427F73 2015   jC813'.6   C2014-900833-3
                                                      C2014-900834-1

Edited by Sue Tate
Designed by Ron Lightburn and Andrew Roberts
The artwork in this book was created using acrylic paint on 300 lb hot press watercolor paper.
The text was set in Superhero.
www.tundrabooks.com

Printed and bound in China

1 2 3 4 5 6   20 19 18 17 16 15

FRANKENSTINK!

GARBAGE GONE BAD

by

RON LIGHTBURN

TUNDRA
BOOKS

Remember that **stuff** on the floor of your room?
The **junk** that is never swept up with a broom?
The scraps that your mom tries to throw in the trash?
The treasures you hoard for your own private stash?

The toys you forget or kick under the bed?
The spider that lives on the teddy bear's head?
The T-shirts and sneakers and greasy old chips?
The chocolate-bar wrappers and cola-drink drips?

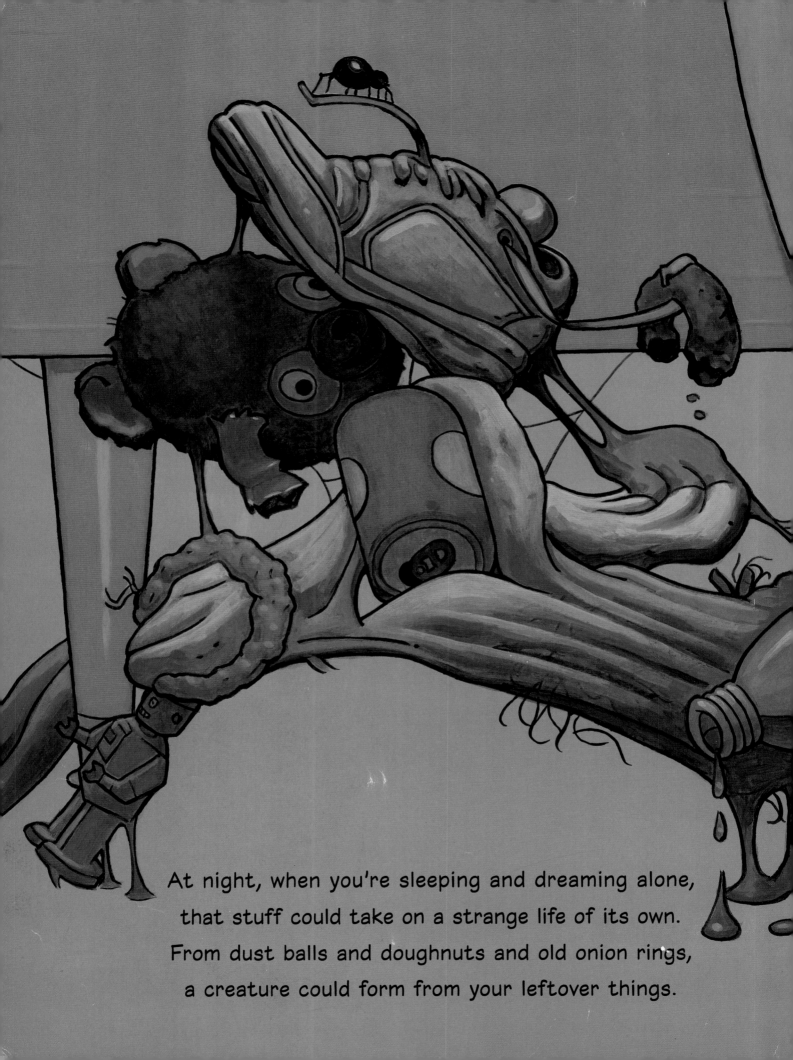

At night, when you're sleeping and dreaming alone,
that stuff could take on a strange life of its own.
From dust balls and doughnuts and old onion rings,
a creature could form from your leftover things.

A slithering **BLOB** that is all stuck together,
with gum wads as tough and as tasteless as leather.
But what is the **SPARK** for this magical potion?
What is the secret to set it in motion?

A **SMELL** that ignites this revolting development?
A **STINK** that creates an alarming experiment?
Like **FARTS** that get trapped under blankets and sheets?
Or **BURPS** that you belch from those sliced pickled beets?
Or moldy green crumbs in an old cracker box?
That torn pair of undies or yesterday's socks?

Or maybe because you skipped out on your bath
(since you hate soaping up more than spelling or math)
and the pillow is stuck to your sweaty bad hair
while the window is shut, keeping out the fresh air?
So you **toss** and you **turn** in the hot stuffy night,
and the temperature makes the conditions just right ...

This thing comes to life and proceeds to the door,
with all of its parts rising up from the floor.
Its skin is all greasy with bubble-gum boils,
oozing with ketchup and three kinds of oils.

A creepy concoction that **w r i g g l e s** around
leaving a trail of slick slime on the ground.
It slides down the hall and peers into the kitchen.
Its hunger is growin', its belly is twitchin'.

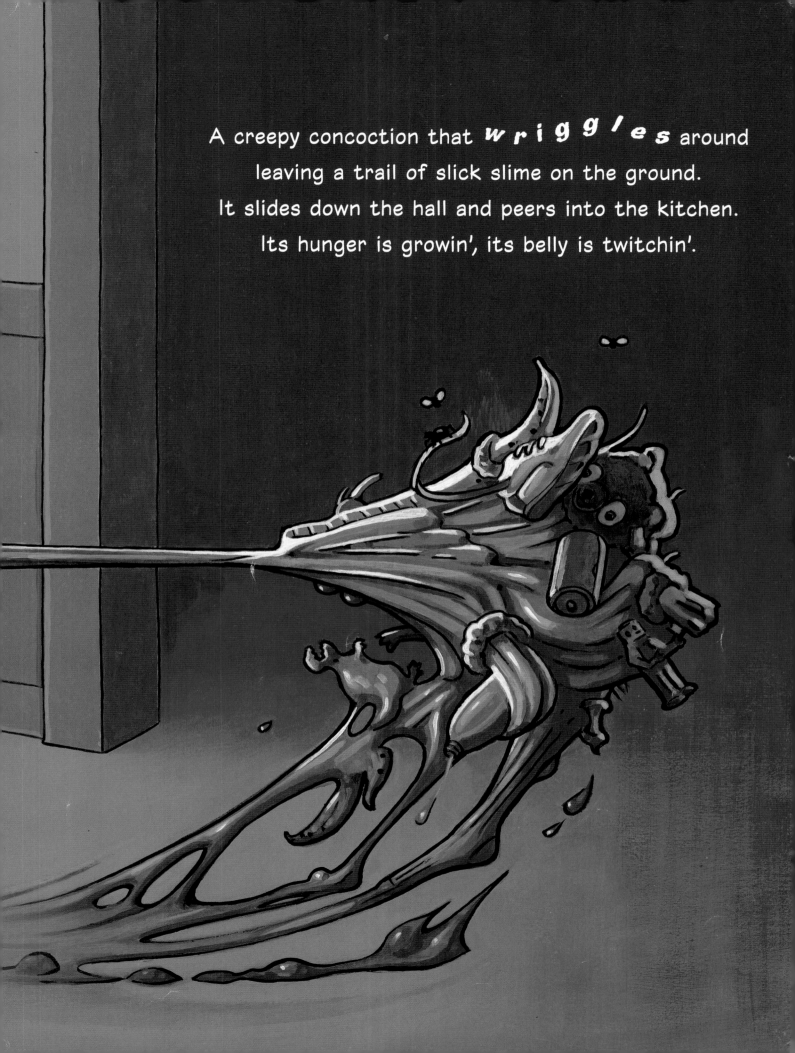

It opens the fridge and it catches a whiff
of some leftover lunch that it snarfs with a sniff.
It empties each bottle, each box and each bag,
with a gross-sounding **GULP** and a gurgling **GAG**.

In slide the carrots and sugar snap peas,
with a dollop of mustard and chunks of old cheese.
Down go the peppers, the pickles and pop,
with a *fizzy* farewell and a crunchy **KERPLOP!**

And when it has gobbled each plum, peach and pear,
the fruit bowl is empty, the cupboards are bare.
Now that it's finished, its body has grown.
It peers out the window and lets out a *moan*.

It spies our green garbage bags stacked by the street,
stuffed full of food scraps and last week's old meat.
Its stomach is growling, its senses are quivering.
Just seeing those bags sets its body **A-SHIVERING**.

The garbage-bag contents are soon gobbled up
with a **BURP** and a **BELCH** and hearty **HICCUP**.
The neighbors have also got garbage bags stacked
with more tempting treats, as a matter of fact.

The bags form a trail that can't be ignored.
They make a delectable trash smorgasbord.
With each stack of bags, it moves more out of sight,
a ravenous wretch rolling into the night.

The goal of this lumbering, loathsome, large lump
is the Graveyard of Garbage –

This landscape of rubbish provides a great feast
for the resident rats and, now, for the beast.
A mountainous salad of plastic and **GOO,**
fast-food leftovers and Styrofoam stew.

Greedily gorging on acres of gunk,
the thing is mutating with each tasty chunk.

Towering higher, it keeps getting fatter,
with a crunching and sucking and slobbering clatter.
It blocks out the sky like a big bloated toad.
If it takes one more bite, it is sure to

EXPLODE!

Then, all of a sudden, it's starting to **SHAKE.**
It seems that last gulp was a big fat mistake.
With a **RUMBLE** and **ROAR** like a volcanic blast,
the thing has erupted ... and eaten its last.

Up goes the waste with a whopping **KASPLOOEY!**
Down come the pieces all smelly and gooey.

With a squish and a squash and a queasy **KERPLUNK**
rains a shower of bits of gelatinous junk.

And all over town are a million small lumps
of gross globs of **GOO** that collect into clumps.
They attract and absorb any stray bits of stuff
before coming to life with a **FART** or a **FLUFF**.

In the warmth of the sun, they will simmer and sizzle,
bubbling up with a **POP** and a **FIZZLE**.
And then, before long, they will all start to grow.
You'll wake up one morning and holler,

"OH NO!"

So compost those scraps on the floor of your closet.
Take back those bottles and get the deposit!
Break out the polish, the bleach and the mop.
Sweep up those hair balls and wipe up that slop!
Get out that vacuum and clean up your lair.
Do all your laundry and shampoo your hair!

And maybe if you change the way that you think,
you won't have to worry about